D.E. Mills

Presents

Little Dribble and the Flow of Water

Hello,

this is a cloud.

Above the ground, deep in his belly,

there was a party in his tummy.

Little Dribble and all his friends

laughed and sang and played within.

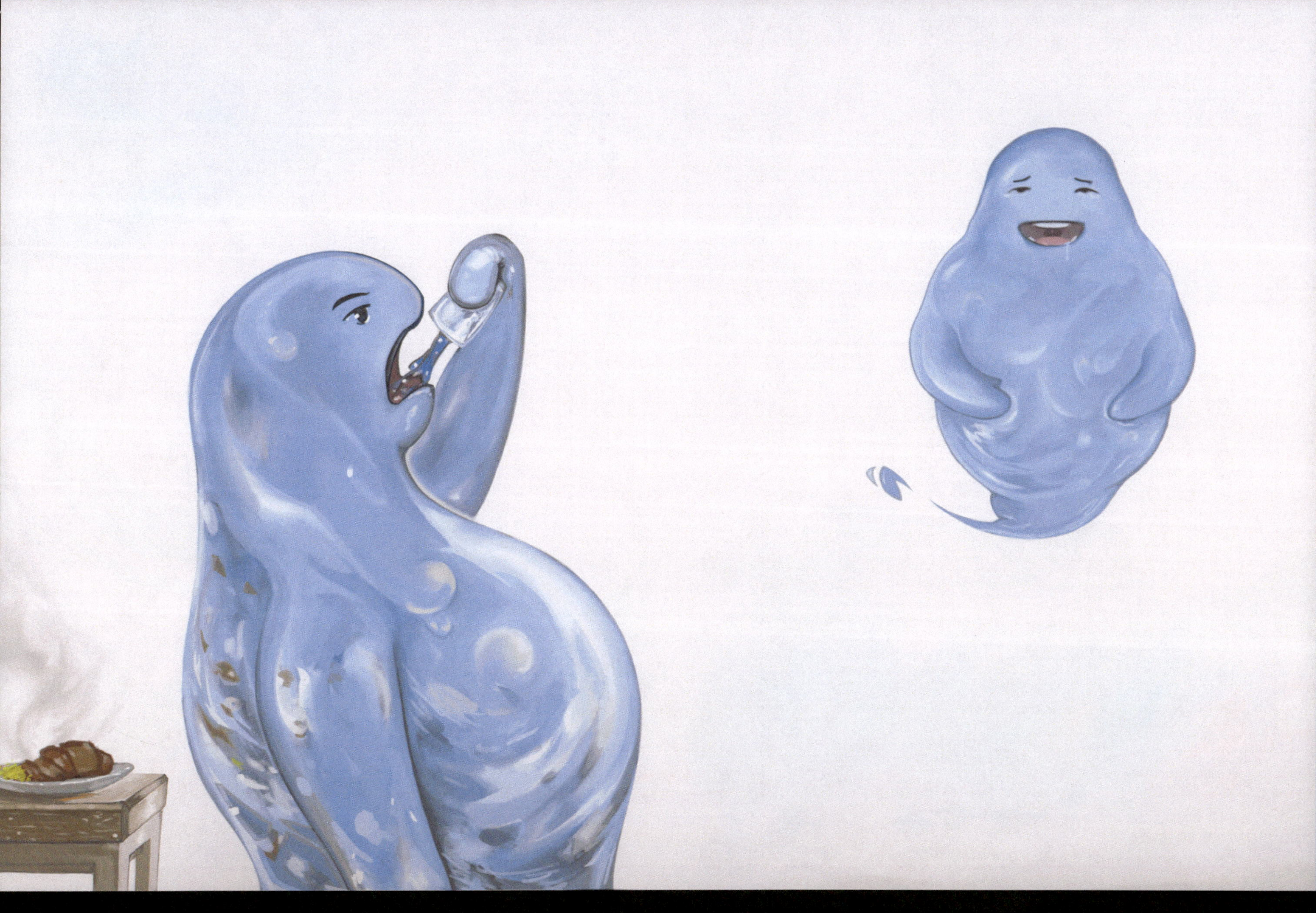

They ate and drank and grew real big,

then bigger, and BIGGER,

until they slipped!

They yelled and yelled,

and fell and fell,

frightened, they hit with a *splish!*

It's okay, because it's rain.

Little Dribble dripped down the drain.

Through the gutters and up the river,

he saw so much that made him shiver.

Before long,

the water calmed,

and Little Dribble was all alone.

He looked around and
then cried out,

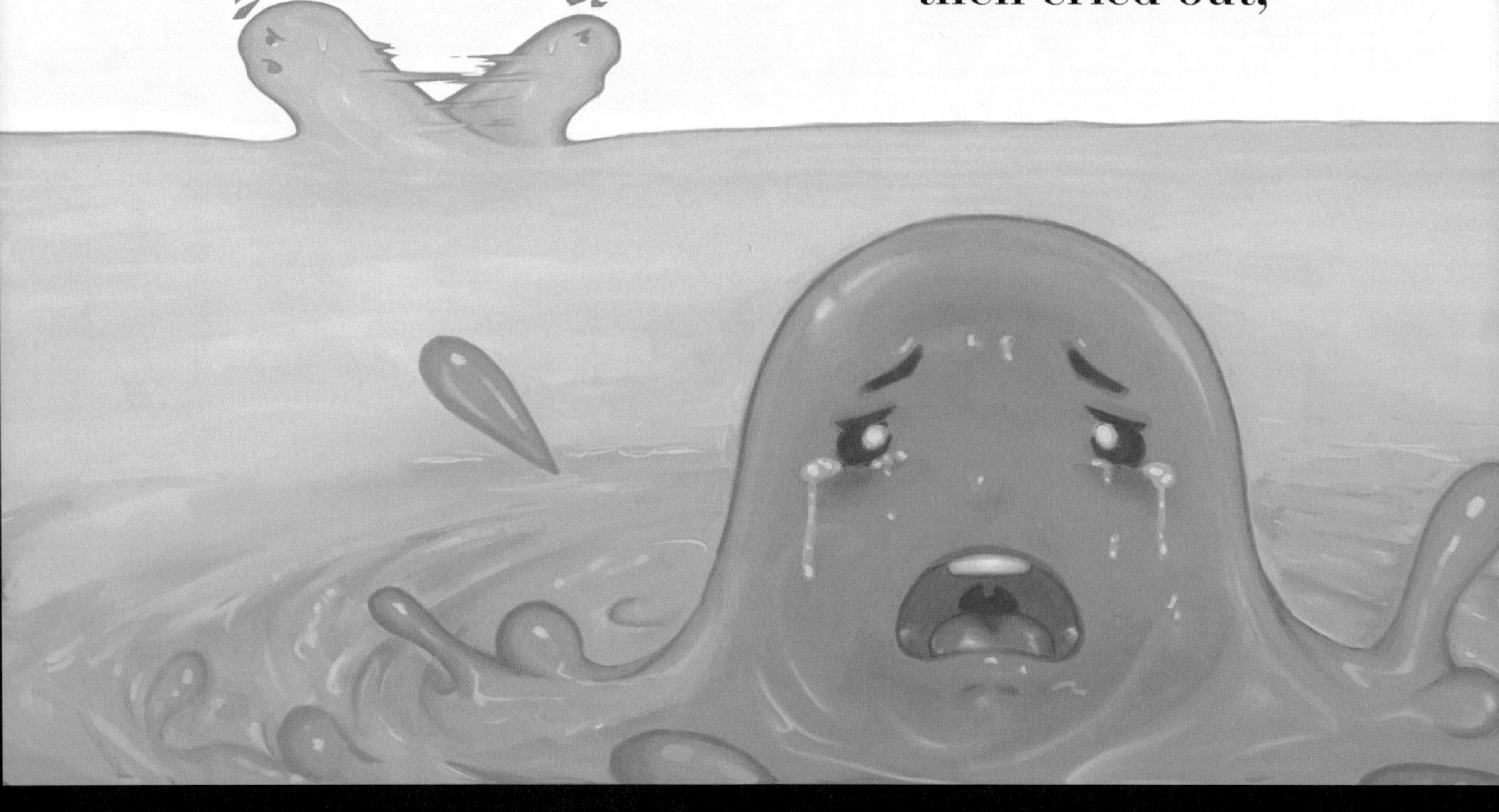

Then the sun came out with shining rays,

He got higher,

and higher, and then…

he found himself surrounded by friends.

The End

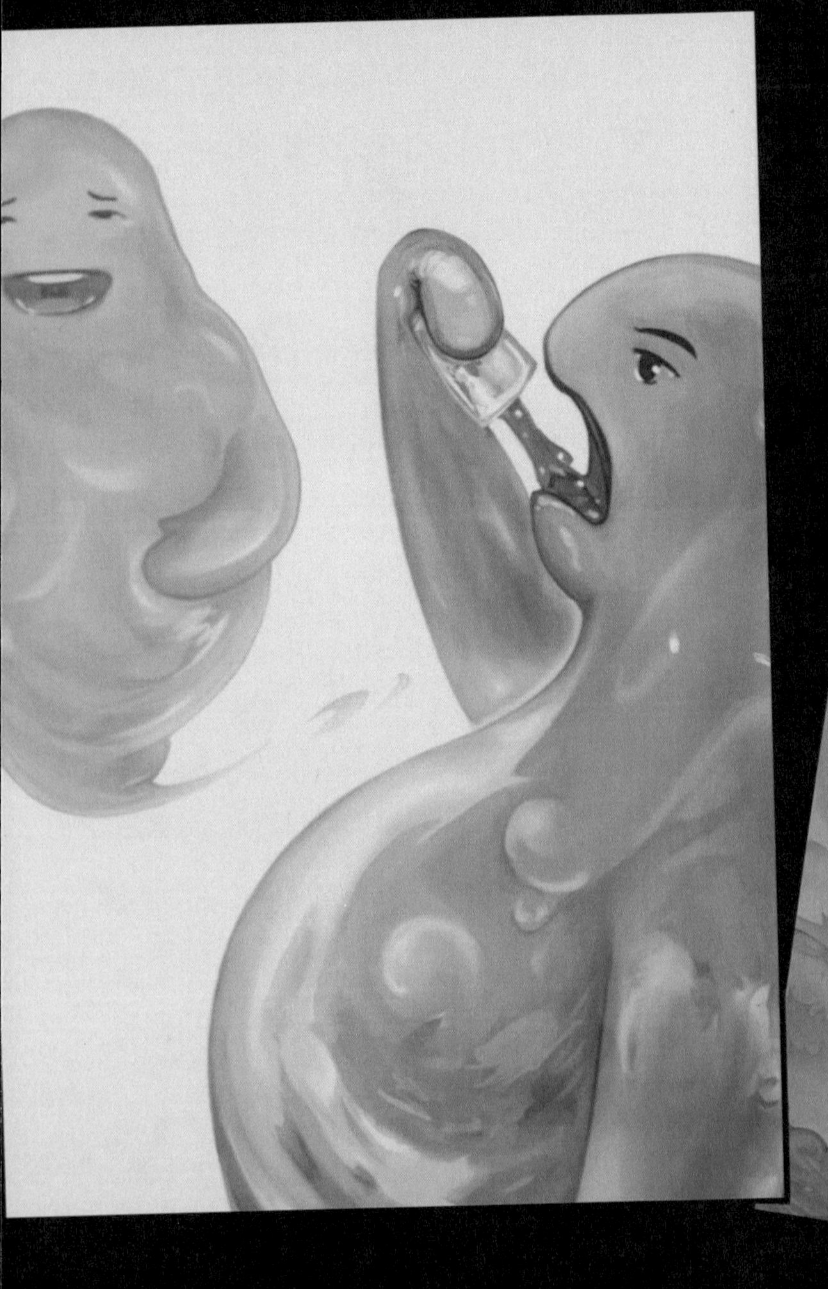

Thanks For Reading!

www.ingramcontent.com/pod-product-compliance
Lightning Source LLC
Chambersburg PA
CBRC091104300726
48978CB00010B/191